LITTLENOSE MOVES HOUSE

Littlenose's home was a cave. When he was alive, a long, long time ago, all respectable families lived like that. So when it rained so much one day that the cave got flooded, they had to move out, then search for a new cave. At last, Father found the perfect cave – but there was one big problem. It was already occupied by three large, fierce bears.

How Littlenose played his part in saving the new family home is just one of his adventures in this book.

Littlenose was invented for John Grant's own children, but was soon entertaining millions more when he first appeared on Jackanory in 1968.

The Neanderthal boy whose pet was bought in a mammoth sale, whose mother is in despair at the rough treatment he gives his furs, and whose exasperated father sometimes threatens to feed him to a sabre-toothed tiger, is everybody's favourite.

Besides gaining wide acceptance in Great Britain, the Littlenose stories have been translated into German, French, Italian, Dutch, Spanish and Japanese.

LITTLENOSE
MOVES HOUSE

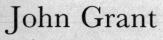

John Grant

Illustrated by the author

BBC/KNIGHT

Copyright © John Grant 1969
First published 1969 by the British Broadcasting Corporation
*This edition published 1984 by the British Broadcasting
Corporation/Knight Books*

Second impression 1984

British Library C.I.P.

Grant, John
   Littlenose moves house.
   I. Title
   823'.914 [J]   PZ7

ISBN 0-340-35335-X

Printed and bound in Great Britain for the British
Broadcasting Corporation, 35 Marylebone High Street,
London W1M 4AA and Hodder and Stoughton
Paperbacks, a division of Hodder and Stoughton Ltd.,
Mill Road, Dunton Green, Sevenoaks, Kent (Editorial
Office: 47 Bedford Square, London, WC1 3DP) by
Richard Clay (The Chaucer Press) Ltd, Bungay, Suffolk

Contents

The Sun Dance

Littlenose was a Neanderthal boy who lived long, long ago. The Neanderthal Folk did not live in houses like us, but in caves. They did not wear clothes like us, but animal furs. They were short and stocky, with enormous noses. Except Littlenose, that is. His nose was only the size of a berry.

The days when Littlenose lived were what we now call the Ice Age because much of the land was hidden under a great mass of ice.

The summers were only *just* warm, and in winter, gales and blizzards swept down from the ice-covered mountains, while the people huddled over roaring fires in their draughty caves and waited for spring.

One cold winter's day when the snow lay thick over everything, and the wind screamed and howled outside the cave, Littlenose was sitting by the fire with his Father and Mother.

Father and Mother were talking together in low voices. "I still think he's too young to be told," said Mother. "He won't understand."

"He's got to know some time," replied Father, "and now is as good a time as any. You wouldn't want him to grow up knowing nothing about it, would you, now?"

He turned to Littlenose, who had been listening with one ear anyway, and said: "Littlenose, you're getting to be a big boy, and there's something you must know. Listen carefully, and I'll explain."

"I still think he's too young," said Mother, but Father gave her a look and went on:

"In summer, the sun is warm. It melts snow, opens the flowers, ripens the fruit and warms the breeze. Now, this is very hard work, and like any hard work, it makes the sun very, very tired. Now, Littlenose, tell me, what happens in autumn when the fruits are ripe?"

"It gets cold," said Littlenose.

"Quite right," said Father, "and have you ever stopped to think why?"

Littlenose, who rarely stopped to think of anything, said, "No."

"Well," continued Father, "I'll tell you. All the effort of making things grow leaves the sun very weak indeed. As the year goes on, it gives out less and less heat. It rises late and sets early, and soon has barely enough strength to rise above the horizon. Just now it is so feeble that you might think that a heavy shower of rain would wipe it out altogether. If the sun is not to die and leave us without light and warmth, then something has to be done every year to keep it going for another summer. So far, you have been too little to take part, but now you will do your bit . . . starting tomorrow. In three days' time is the Sun Dance."

The next three days were very busy for Littlenose, and indeed for the whole tribe.

First of all they worked hard clearing all

the snow from a flat circle of ground among the trees.

Next, they went into the woods and gathered green branches. They found yew and fir, and holly with masses of round, red berries. They cut long streamers of ivy from the rocks and tree trunks. They climbed trees to bring down clusters of bright green mistletoe with white berries, and collected armfuls of dark laurel. From the hillsides they cut sprays of green broom and gorse, the last of which Littlenose didn't like one bit, as it scratched his arms and prickled his fingers. All this greenery was piled in the clearing until there was barely room to move.

But they weren't finished yet.

Some of the men went off into the woods again with their flint axes, and after a great deal of labour re-appeared looking tired but pleased with themselves, and dragging a slender spruce tree. They pulled it into the clearing, and after much effort by everyone,

and a good deal of shouting and confusion, it
was set upright in the ground.

Now everyone began to help decorate the
clearing with the green branches.

The ivy was strung between the tree trunks,
with clusters of holly and mistletoe along
it at intervals. More holly and mistletoe
were entwined with the fir, laurel, gorse and
broom to form wreaths and garlands and

sprays. These were fixed on the bare trunks and branches of the trees until, compared with the bare snow-covered land round about, the clearing began to look like a little bit of summer that had been left over.

"This," explained Father, "is what we are trying to do. We will show the sun what summer is like so that it will remember, and we shall light fires, to warm it and give it back some of its strength. There will also be, of course, singing and feasting and dancing. And we all get presents."

"This," thought Littlenose, "gets better every minute."

The day of the Sun Dance came at last. Littlenose was out early, and anxiously watched the sun as it rose above the hills. It seemed to be hardly moving, but at last the dull red ball was in full view. It didn't look at all healthy, and Littlenose hoped that they weren't going to be too late.

At last, dressed in his best furs, Littlenose set

off with his parents.

The clearing was crowded. Everyone was happy and smiling, but nothing appeared to be happening yet. Then everyone fell silent and looked towards the spruce tree, which was decorated with holly berries, and hung with intriguing bundles. The Old Man, who was the leader of the tribe, was standing by the tree with a lighted torch in his hand, and Littlenose saw that a huge unlit fire had been prepared. The topmost log of the fire was decorated like the trees.

Facing the sun, which was slipping below the horizon, the Old Man began to sing, while the people clapped their hands in time with him. Then everyone gradually joined in, till the sound of singing and clapping

shook the snow from the trees.

Suddenly, the singing and clapping stopped. The Old Man stepped forward, held his torch towards the sun and said something in a loud voice. He said it again, and Littlenose somehow expected the sun to jump back up into the darkening sky.

But it didn't.

The Old Man thrust his torch into the fire, which burst into flames. At the same time, smaller fires around the edge of the clearing were lit. Food was brought out in quantities which made Littlenose's eyes pop with wonder.

First, there was fruit. Crab apples and pears, brown skinned and wrinkled but soft and sweet inside. There were sticky red berries from the dark woods and hips, haws and brambles from the thickets by the river.

There were all manner of nuts. Chestnuts, beechnuts, hazels, walnuts, acorns and even earth-nuts.

Then, from the river, were trout, salmon, crayfish and mussels.

Littlenose could hardly enjoy one thing for hurrying on to the next. He stuffed his mouth full, and for once no one told him to mind his manners.

However, all this time, a crowd of women had been busy around the big fire. A delicious smell began to drift across the clearing. Littlenose, thinking the wonders of the night would never end, went to investigate.

A giant ox was being roasted over the flames. Gravy dripped and sizzled, and the smell nearly drove Littlenose mad with

impatience. The meat was almost ready, and
in a few minutes Littlenose was wolfing down
his share with gusto. With the roast ox were
also served mushrooms, truffles and all kinds
of sweet-tasting roots and bulbs.

Littlenose began to think that perhaps even
he couldn't possibly eat another mouthful,
when pieces of honeycomb were passed round.
The wax was crisp and the honey had turned
partly to sugar. Littlenose crunched and
munched, and thought that he was the happiest
boy in the whole world.

The food was cleared away, and the singing
and dancing began. Everyone clapped the
dancers, who leapt and whirled, pretending to
be birds, animals, hunters, and even fish.

Everyone joined in the singing, and
Littlenose, who didn't know all the songs,
joined in just the same.

When Littlenose was almost nodding with
weariness, the Old Man stood up and everyone
became quiet.

He stood by the decorated spruce tree and
the tribe waited eagerly. Then, one by one,
he called their names. As each person went
forward he was given one of the little bundles
from the tree.

Mother's contained a bone comb. Father
got a new barbed point for his fishing spear.
And Littlenose? He was speechless with
delight. He was given two small flints! He felt
really grown-up. He could light his own
fires now.

And that was almost the end of another Sun Dance.

Just before they returned to their caves, the people all stood, while the Old Man stretched out his arms and cried: "We have had warmth and light and laughter. May the Great Sun grow in strength from day to day and bring us yet another summer."

And, do you know . . . it did!

Two-Eyes' Friends

Littlenose's best friend was Two-Eyes, his pet mammoth. He had bought Two-Eyes at the market when no one else wanted him, and was very fond of him indeed. Two-Eyes was a roly-poly little creature with a trunk, big flapping ears, and a long shaggy coat. When he curled up to sleep at night he looked for all the world like an enormous ball of wool.

But the market was not the only place where mammoths were to be found. Great herds of them roamed the land. They usually kept well clear of the places where people lived, but occasionally, if food were scarce, they would be seen close at hand, and Littlenose had several times watched from a safe distance as a herd went by.

The young mammoths were like Two-Eyes, only as tall as Littlenose himself, but the grown-up ones towered as tall as trees, with long powerful trunks and enormous curved tusks.

One day, Littlenose was playing one of his own very complicated games outside the cave where he lived. It involved twigs and stones and patterns in the sand, and was so intricate that only he really understood it. Two-Eyes, who was supposed to be playing, eventually gave up and wandered away by himself.

He made his way up the hill behind the cave and on to the grassy upland beyond. It was a lovely day, and a fresh wind was blowing.

Two-Eyes snuffed at the breeze with his trunk. It was full of all sorts of interesting smells. He took another snuffle, and his eyes grew round with excitement. His ears spread out and his trunk held straight in front of him, he trotted forward, following an unusual scent. It grew stronger every moment, until he came to the edge of a hollow, and saw something that made him squeal with delight.

It was a huge herd of mammoths!

The great males were standing on the edge of the crowd, keeping watch for any cave lion or sabre-toothed tiger who might fancy a piece of mammoth steak for lunch. The females gathered in groups exchanging mammoth gossip, while there were dozens of young ones, like Two-Eyes, running and jumping and playing all over the place.

Two-Eyes gave a little squeal and trotted down into the hollow. The young mammoths stopped playing and watched him suspiciously. One of them came over to Two-Eyes. They snuffled at each other and grunted and squeaked in mammoth talk, and a moment later were firm friends. The others crowded round, and they too squeaked and grunted at Two-Eyes, and soon it was as if they had known each other all their lives.

Then the games started again. They ran races, played tug-of-war with their trunks, and did a wonderful dance. Each held the tail of the one in front in his trunk, while they wound their way in a long snaky line through the hollow, much to the annoyance of the grown-ups.

Two-Eyes was enjoying himself so much that he forgot the time. Only when the sun was getting low in the sky did he realize that it was late, and that he ought to be thinking of going home.

He trumpeted "Good-bye" to his friends and started to leave. But they didn't want him to go! They came running after him, and crowded round, while Two-Eyes desperately tried to explain that he *had* to go.

They would come too, they squealed; and Two-Eyes couldn't make them understand that he lived in a cave with Littlenose and his Mother and Father. The mammoths didn't want to be parted from their new friend, and in the end, Two-Eyes set off with them all crowding round him.

Meanwhile, Littlenose had realized that Two-Eyes had not returned, and it was getting near bedtime. He stood at the cave entrance and called: "TWO-EYES!"

But there was no answer.

He called again, and was just about to set
off to look for him in the woods when, looking
up, he saw a black shape appear on the crest
of the hill behind the cave. "Come on,
Two-Eyes," he shouted. "It's late. Almost
bedtime."

The black shape started running down the
hill, and Littlenose was about to turn away
when he gasped in horror. Not one, but
dozens of little black mammoths were coming
over the the crest. Like a black, furry wave
they poured over and down, heading straight
for the cave. Littlenose turned to run . . . but
he was too late.

The mammoths swept past and over him,
knocking him off his feet. In a cloud of dust,
and squealing and snorting, they rushed
straight into the cave.

Pots broke, the supper was trampled underfoot, the fire was stamped out . . . and Mother and Father were pushed flat up against the back of the cave.

Mother was speechless . . . but Father wasn't!

"LITTLENOSE!" he screamed. "Get them out! This is all your fault! Get these stupid creatures out before they knock the whole place down!"

Littlenose got safely behind a tree this time before he called: "TWO-EYES!"

Two-Eyes heard and came running out of the cave . . . but so did all the others. Once more the black furry tide swept around Littlenose, but this time it didn't knock him down.

"Please, Two-Eyes," said Littlenose, "I don't know which one is you. Couldn't you please ask your friends to go home, and only *you* come when I call?"

But of course the friends didn't want to go. They stood, pressed close around Littlenose, waiting to see what would happen next. They were enjoying this new game.

In the cave, Father and Mother looked at the damage. It was dreadful. There was hardly a thing that hadn't been broken.

"That mammoth is the stupidest creature I know," said Father, angrily.

"I'm sure he didn't mean it," said Mother, soothingly, "he was only playing with his friends. He's brought them visiting, and they want to meet us."

"Well," said Father, "they won't get a second chance," and he began to block up the entrance with rocks, leaving only a space at one side.

"Come on, Littlenose," he called. "Hurry, or you'll be locked out."

"But I can't come without Two-Eyes," Littlenose wailed. "He can't stay out all night, and . . . I don't know which *is* Two-Eyes. They *all* answer when I call."

"Two-Eyes should have thought of that before he started all this foolishness," called back Father. "Now hurry. It's getting dark."

Littlenose was desperate. He just couldn't leave Two-Eyes out all night, but how was he to tell which one *was* his pet?

Then he remembered. Of course! How silly could he get? Two-Eyes got his name because his eyes were different colours . . . one red and one green. Other mammoths had *two* red eyes, all Littlenose had to do was look.

It took ages. The mammoths' long shaggy fur hung down over their eyes, and he had to go round each one, stroking it and carefully parting the fur over its eyes to see the colour. He had looked at more than half before he found Two-Eyes.

Father was making very impatient gestures from the cave, so Littlenose quickly leaned over and whispered in Two-Eyes' ear: "Do as I tell you, Two-Eyes, and go very slowly. We don't want this lot charging into the cave again. Now, come along."

Taking Two-Eyes' trunk in his hand, he led him slowly through the closely crowded mammoths. Those in front made way for them, while those behind fell in to make a sort of procession. Gradually, they drew nearer to the cave. Littlenose let go of the trunk, and began to steer Two-Eyes from behind, aiming at the gap in the barricade.

Then, just as Two-Eyes' head was in the
cave, Littlenose gave him an enormous push,
while at the same time he whirled round with
a yell and waved his arms.

Two-Eyes scrambled into the cave, while
the mammoths scattered in all directions.
Littlenose jumped inside, and Father quickly
blocked the opening.

All night the little creatures cried and
whimpered outside for their friend.
Occasionally, a small trunk would poke
through a chink in the rocks, and no one got a
wink of sleep.

However, just before daybreak, they heard the most dreadful noise. There were loud trumpetings and crashings and the thunder of many great feet. Father peeped out.

"It's the mammoths!" he cried. "They've come for their young."

34

The adults were very angry with the young
ones for running away, and were slapping
and spanking them with their trunks while
chasing them home. The loud noises went on
for a long time, but eventually died away in
the distance.

In the morning, everything looked a bit
flattened, but otherwise there was no sign of
the mammoth herd.

Later in the day Littlenose climbed up to
the hollow. But the mammoths had gone from
there too, and although in the following weeks
Two-Eyes visited the hollow hopefully, they
never came back.

The Painted Cave

In the days when Littlenose lived, men painted
pictures on the walls of caves. In some parts of
the world, you can still see the pictures they
made. They show mammoths, deer, horses
and rhinoceros, as well as men hunting
and women dancing.

However, it was not Littlenose's people, the
Neanderthal folk, who painted the caves.
They occasionally might scratch a rough
outline of a lion or a hyena on a bone or
piece of stone, and Littlenose sometimes made
pictures in the wet sand or in the dust, but
the secret of mixing colours and making
lifelike drawings of animals belonged to the
Straightnoses.

Now, the Straightnoses didn't live

respectably in caves, they were wanderers, living out in the open. But they were great hunters, and part of their success in hunting lay in *magic!* And this was why they painted the caves. These caves were very special and secret places, only visited by the hunters and leaders of the Straightnose tribes. If they were planning a deer hunt, say, they would come to the cave and perform magical dances and sing spells and enchantments before a picture of a deer, and this ensured that the hunt would be successful.

Littlenose, of course, knew nothing of all this.

One day, he and Two-Eyes, with Mother and Father, were far from home. Father had heard of a place where flints could be dug out of the ground, which was cheaper than buying them; and so, armed with a pick fashioned from a deer's antler, they had set off before daylight. Now, Father was banging and hacking away at the chalky hillside in a great cloud of white dust, and had already unearthed some first class flints.

Two-Eyes, as usual, had gone to sleep, while Mother was preparing a picnic lunch.

Littlenose had discovered a small stream, and was playing one of his favourite games, that of dropping twigs into the water and watching them sail along until they were out of sight. After a while, he thought it would be fun to follow the twigs and see where they went.

The stream had cut itself a deep channel, and, after a short distance, the grass and bushes grew right over to form a green tunnel.

Littlenose ran after the twigs, and
under the green arch. It was rather exciting,
and he hurried splashing along. Suddenly,
he noticed that it had become darker. He
looked up. The sides of the tunnel were
still earth and rock but so was the roof. He
looked back. He had been so busy watching
his twigs that he hadn't noticed that the
stream had left the open and was flowing into
a dark hole in the ground.

Forgetting all his Father's warnings about going into strange caves, Littlenose decided to explore. He splashed into the tunnel, which was just high enough for him to stand upright. It was fairly straight, and enough light came in for him to see by. He kept glancing behind him, and decided he would turn back when he could no longer see the entrance. On he went. It was chilly and dark and he disturbed several bats which went fluttering and twittering past his head.

Then the tunnel turned sharp right. Littlenose hesitated, looked back at the light for a moment, and carried on.

Immediately, he could see light ahead of him.

"It must be the end," thought Littlenose.

But it wasn't a bit like sunlight. It was flickering and yellow, and also the stream was beginning to run faster and to make a loud splashing sound up ahead.

Littlenose splashed the last few yards . . . and stopped in amazement.

The tunnel did not end in daylight.

It stopped high up in the side of a huge cavern, while the stream splashed its way down the rock face and into a dark pool at the foot. The cavern was lit by a number of torches made of pine branches stuck into cracks in the rock. But, most remarkable of all, the walls were covered with pictures.

Now, occasionally, Littlenose did very silly things, and he ought to have known that a

cave that had pictures *and* torches burning
must belong to *someone*; but, without hesitation,
he scrambled down the rocks and ran to have
a closer look.

He had never seen anything like it before.
There were pictures of mammoth herds,
galloping horses, charging bulls, and a whole
party of hunters with spears. There was one
particular picture of a huge bison which looked
very new. In fact, the paint looked still wet . . .
and Littlenose patted it with his hand to make
sure. Of course, it *was* wet, and Littlenose got
paint all over the palm of his hand, but he
cleaned it off on the rock, leaving red hand

prints, then wiped his hand on his furs.

He was still admiring the pictures when he heard the oddest sound. He turned, and cocked his head to listen. He just couldn't think what it was, but it was rather frightening, and it was getting louder. He stood still where he was until he realized that it was voices he was hearing. Men's voices, echoing among the rocks!

Littlenose scrambled, for dear life, up the rocks to his tunnel, and watched.

The noise was almost deafening when, from an opening at the opposite side of the cave a long line of men came marching. At least,

Littlenose thought they were men. They walked upright, but their bodies were covered with strange coloured patterns. Some of them even appeared to have animals' heads! But it was the leader who was the most ferocious. He was the most hideously painted, and his head was hidden under a great mass of shaggy hair from which protruded two sharp bison horns. In each hand he carried a long, red-pointed spear.

The procession halted in front of the newly-painted bison. Some men squatted in a semi-circle with short sticks in their hands. The rest stood behind, while the leader stood facing them with his arms outstretched.

The men started clapping their hands and beating their sticks together, and the leader tossed his bison horns and began to dance, while singing in a high-pitched voice. More men joined in the dance, which became fast and furious, while all joined in the singing which rang and echoed around the cave.

Faster grew the dancing, and louder the singing. They whirled, spun and leapt, the flickering torches casting a weird light and making the painted animals seem almost alive. Littlenose leaned forward in excitement.

The dancers had fallen back, now, and the leader was alone in front of the bison. The singing stopped as he raised his spears.

Littlenose leaned further forward.

His hand touched a loose rock.

With a resounding splash, it toppled into the pool.

Instantly, the crowd turned as one man. The leader pointed up at Littlenose and screamed.

Littlenose fled!

Back along the tunnel he splashed and stumbled.

Shouting and screaming, his pursuers scrambled up the rocks. They were so anxious to catch him that they climbed over each other in their haste, and some missed their footing and fell head first into the pool.

Littlenose looked back as he ran. He was leaving his pursuers behind. He could run upright, but they had to bend low, and kept banging their heads on the rocky roof and stumbling in the stream.

He reached the corner and looked back again.

The Straightnoses had given up, and had gone back to their interrupted dance.

Littlenose hurried to where the daylight shone through the over-hanging leaves, and out into the open air. He sat down on the grass for a moment to get his breath back, then set off to rejoin his parents . . . wondering what on earth Mother would say when she saw the red paint on his good furs.

After the Straightnoses had finished their magic dance, one might think that they would be very annoyed at the mess Littlenose had made with the paint, and would clean his hand-marks off the wall. But, in the caves in Lascaux, in France, you can see not only lots of beautifully painted animals, but, if you look carefully, a number of hand-prints.

Could they be Littlenose's, do you think?

The Giant Snowball

Littlenose, like all boys, loved the snow, and
in the days when he lived there was usually
snow to be found somewhere at all times of
the year. Two-Eyes was not so fond of it. He
would join Littlenose in sliding sometimes,
but he objected to the way in which the snow
caught in his fur and formed into icicles. Then,
when he went home, Mother would be angry
as the ice melted and dripped water all over the
floor.

One cold winter's day, the snow lay thick
and smooth over the land. Littlenose, bundled
up in his winter furs, was playing one of his
favourite games. He was following tracks in
the snow. This could be dangerous, because
Littlenose sometimes made mistakes, and had

once followed what he thought was a red deer,
only to find himself suddenly face to face with
a sabre-toothed tiger!

Today, he was following what he hoped
was a moose, and as usual Two-Eyes was
walking behind, pausing from time to time
to shake the snow from his coat, and give
disgusted little snorts through his trunk.

The tracks were clear, and led through
woods, over frozen marshland and up a long

hill. Here, however, he lost them. The top
of the hill was bare and rocky, and the snow
had drifted clear. There was just no way of
telling which way the moose had gone.

With a sigh of relief, Two-Eyes shook
himself once more, then began to clean his
fur with his trunk. Having done this, he
found a sheltered spot behind a rock, and
settled down for a quiet snooze.

Littlenose, meanwhile, was doing some
exploring. Down the hill a little way there was
a wood, and he thought there might be
something interesting to see there.

But it was just an ordinary wood. Then he
found the dead tree. It had been struck by
lightning and stood bare and broken. The
bark had come off in great pieces, and as
Littlenose looked, he had a wonderful idea.
There was one piece of bark which was longer
than Littlenose himself, and quite broad. It
wasn't very heavy, and he was able to drag it
across the ground. He pulled it out from under

the trees and on to the snowy hillside.

Very carefully, he sat down on the piece of
bark – and nothing happened. He pushed
with his hands, and it moved a little. He
pushed again, and it moved a little further.
With all his might, Littlenose leaned back
and heaved. The bark shot forward and next
moment he was careering down the hill.

Littlenose clung hard. He had no idea how
to steer, but he laughed and shouted as his
sledge bounced over the snow.

At last, with a thump, he hit a grassy
tussock, and went somersaulting through

the air. He landed in a deep drift, and scrambled to his feet, brushing the snow out of his hair.

He was amazed to find how far he had travelled. The wood, and the rock where he he had left Two-Eyes, seemed very far away.

It was growing late, and Littlenose knew he ought to start for home, but he wanted just one more ride on his sledge. He looked up at the opposite slope. "If I start from up *there*," he thought, "I'll not only go faster because it's steeper, but maybe a good way up towards the wood if I'm lucky," and he began to drag the piece of bark over the snow.

He was quite out of breath when he reached the top, and stopped for a moment to get his wind back.

Suddenly, he heard something. He wasn't sure what. Perhaps it was only the wind. He heard it again, but louder, and shivered with fright as he realized what it was.

On a ridge some distance away an animal appeared. It threw back its head and howled.

A wolf!

Almost immediately, a whole pack appeared. With one accord, *they* threw back *their* heads and howled, and came trotting across the snow.

Littlenose was terrified. He looked wildly around him for Two-Eyes, but he was far away, up on the opposite hill, beyond the wood.

In a panic, Littlenose turned and threw himself full-length on his piece of bark. It shot forward, and next moment he was hurtling down the hill with the wolf pack in pursuit.

The snow blew up his nose and down his neck, but he didn't care. He lay flat, clinging on for all he was worth, while he bumped and rocked over the hummocky snow.

He glanced back over his shoulder.

The wolves were streaming down the hill, ears back and long red tongues hanging out. Occasionally, one would give a blood-curdling

howl, and take an enormous leap forward.

However, the snow was deep for running, and Littlenose drew slowly ahead. He was almost at the foot of the hill now, and he wondered how far up the opposite side his speed would carry him. He wondered if Two-Eyes would see him from beyond the wood. He craned his neck and tried to see the little mammoth, and was so busy doing this that he didn't see a large rock straight ahead.

The sledge hit the rock with a crash, throwing Littlenose head over heels, and splintering into a thousand pieces of bark.

Littlenose, unhurt, rolled over and over. The wolves, with joyful howls, ran even faster at the thought of a boy for supper.

Littlenose scrambled up. The wolves were
almost on him, and he was a long way from
the top. He began running towards an
enormous fallen pine tree. With the pack at
his heels, he snatched up a thick tree branch
and pulled himself up on to the roots of the
fallen tree.

He was not a moment too soon.

The leading wolf sprang up with snapping
jaws, and Littlenose brought the branch down
hard on its nose. Yelping, it dropped back, but
another came, and then another, until
Littlenose was slashing and swiping as hard
as he could.

He swung his branch once more, and was almost dragged down as a wolf seized it in his jaws and snatched it from him.

Now he had nothing.

But there was a lot of snow lying on the tree-trunk, and Littlenose quickly made a snowball and threw it hard. It caught a wolf in the open jaws, sending it coughing and choking away.

He threw more and more snowballs until he had almost used up all the snow.

Then the wolves drew back. Most of them had sore heads or bloody noses, and they held a council of war to decide what should be done next.

High on the hill, Two-Eyes had wakened from
his nap. His fur was dry, and he felt rather
hungry. It must be time to go home. He
looked around him for Littlenose.

Then he heard the commotion from the foot
of the hill. He couldn't see, but it sounded as
if Littlenose were up to something. Having
got his fur clean, he wasn't very anxious
to venture on to the snowy hillside, but he
carefully picked his way down to the wood.

The noise was much further on, and
Two-Eyes pushed his way through the trees.
The moment he saw Littlenose surrounded by
the wolves, he forgot all about the snow and
his fur.

He put down his head and *charged!*

But he had only taken a few paces before
he realized that the slope was steeper than
he had thought. He was running much too
fast, and before he could stop himself he lost
his footing and tumbled over and over.

Meanwhile, the wolves had decided to have

one more attempt at catching Littlenose. The leader gave a howl, and the whole pack leapt forward. They were met by Littlenose's few remaining snowballs, and were almost upon him when suddenly they stopped.

They were all looking up the hill, although Littlenose couldn't see anything for the branches of the tree. Then one wolf gave a yelp and turned and ran with its tail between its legs. The rest followed, and Littlenose saw why. An enormous snowball was bounding down the hill! Littlenose had never seen anything like it, and neither had the wolves. They fled madly before it, but not before several had been bowled over and sent flying through the air.

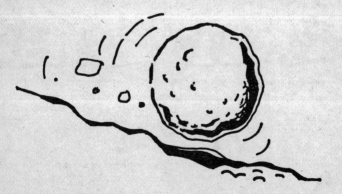

The snowball hurtled on, and the wolves, scrambling over each other in panic, dashed madly away until their howling died in the distance. The snowball rolled a few more yards, then hit a birch sapling and burst apart in a great shower of snow.

Sitting in the middle was Two-Eyes.

"Two-Eyes," shouted Littlenose, "how clever of you! You arrived just in time."

But Two-Eyes wasn't feeling particularly clever. He was so dizzy he could hardly stand. Littlenose took his trunk in his hand and, with Two-Eyes leaving a very wiggly line of footprints in the snow, they set off for home.

Littlenose Moves House

One evening, just as Littlenose was going to
bed, it started to rain. Not much at first, just
a few drops; but soon it was pouring down,
drumming on the hard ground, and splashing
through the cave door to hiss and splutter
in the fire. Late in the night, Littlenose woke
up and listened. The drumming had changed
to a wet splashing as the ground turned to mud,
and several long trickles of water began to ooze
their way across the sandy floor.

By morning the rain had stopped, and after
breakfast Littlenose and Two-Eyes ran
outside to play. They stopped in amazement.
The river, which was usually clear and slow-
flowing, and narrow enough to wade right
across, was roaring past, dark and muddy, with

waves breaking on it . . . and what's more, it was only a few paces from the cave!

A group of men was standing by the water's edge, looking very worried.

"If there's no more rain, it'll start going down by mid-day," said one of them hopefully.

"I'm not so sure," said Father, and he took a stout stick and stood it upright in the soft earth close to where the brown water lapped on the grass. "If it comes no higher than that," he said, "we're all right. Otherwise, we're in trouble!"

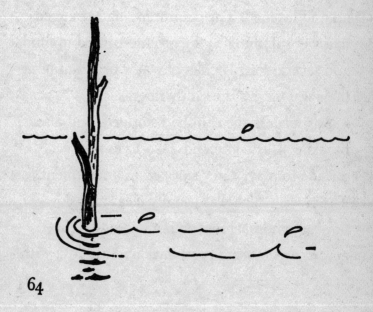

Littlenose decided to keep watch on the
stick . . . and he did for at least five minutes.
Then he grew bored and ran off to play with
Two-Eyes.

By mid-day, the stick was half covered by
the water, and by night-fall it was out of
sight. Several families had already had to
leave their caves and join others more
fortunate in living on higher ground.

In the morning, the Old Man, who was the
leader of the tribe, called them together.
"There has been no rain for a whole day,"
he said, "but still the river rises. We don't

know why, but I am sending out parties of hunters to investigate."

The hunters set off immediately, and had returned by lunch-time. Their story was quickly told. Downstream, the river flowed through a narrow gorge before plunging over a high waterfall. The heavy rain had loosened the earth and rocks, which had crashed down into the gorge, bringing trees and bushes with them, and forming a huge solid dam across the river. The falls were only a trickle now, and behind the dam a new lake was already forming. The whole valley would soon be under water.

The Old Man called the tribe together again.

"There is no time to be lost," he told them. "We must move out of the valley before another rainstorm drowns us all in our caves. We will have to camp out, and each family will be responsible for finding itself a new cave."

Next day, the whole tribe packed its goods and chattels and made camp on the grassy uplands above the valley. Father chose a clump of birch trees, and hung skins and furs between the trunks to make a rough tent. Littlenose was very excited by the whole affair, and ran round and round the tent shrieking with delight.

He annoyed Mother, who shouted at him: "Littlenose, just because we're living like Straightnoses, there's no need to act like one!"

Littlenose crept quietly away. He didn't like being called a Straightnose. They were wandering people of whom the Neanderthal Folk were very much afraid . . . but also very scornful. The Straightnoses did not live respectably in caves, but camped in the open and followed the animal herds.

Father and Mother started house hunting as soon as they were settled in their camp. Every morning they set out, leaving Littlenose with strict orders about not playing with the fire and not straying from the camp. And every evening they returned tired and weary without having found anything. At last, one day Mother told Father to go by himself. She said she'd had enough of poking about unsuitable caves, and a day at home would do her no harm.

So Father set off.

It was late when he returned, but he looked very pleased with himself.

"Well," said Father, "I've found it. We leave in the morning."

"What's it like?" said Mother, eagerly.

Father, looking very pompous, drew himself up and recited: "An attractive detached family residence comprising a dry, well-ventilated cave conveniently situated near fresh water, fire-wood etc. Immediate entry by arrangement with present owners."

"Who are the present owners?" asked Mother.

"Bears," said Father. "Three bears. We leave at dawn tomorrow, and in two days' time we should be settled in our new home."

Littlenose slept very little that night. He lay and tossed and turned and fidgeted, keeping everyone else awake, so that they were really very glad when the sky turned pink, and it was time to pack.

After breakfast, Mother and Father busied themselves with bundling up their belongings and loading up Two-Eyes, who was to carry his share.

Littlenose wandered away and looked down into the valley. The water stretched from side to side and as far as he could see. There was no sign of the old cave. He wondered if perhaps some day another rain-storm might wash away the landslide at the gorge, and let them return to their old home.

"Come on, Littlenose, it's time to go," called Father.

They set off, Father leading the way with

his club in his hand. Mother came next
carrying a large bundle on her head, and
Two-Eyes brought up the rear, almost
hidden under the enormous pile of furs, pots,
and odds and ends slung on his back. Littlenose
was everywhere at once. He darted back and
forth chasing butterflies. He stopped to pick
flowers . . . then threw them away to chase
rabbits. Father and Mother grew very
annoyed with him as he ran in front of them,
bumped into them, and got in the way
generally. However, by the time they stopped
to eat at noon, Littlenose had tired himself
out, and was content to continue the journey
walking quietly beside Two-Eyes.

Night was falling when Father held his
hand up as a signal to stop, and Littlenose sat
wearily on the grass.

Before them, the land sloped gently away.
It was grassy with occasional large trees, and
just visible in the dusk was a broad, slowly-
flowing river.

Father pointed down the slope. "There it is," he said, and Littlenose and Mother saw, partly hidden by some trees, and back from the river, a great tumbled mass of rocks.

"In there," said Father, "is as snug and cosy a cave as you could imagine."

"What about the bears?" asked Mother.

"We wait here until they go out for their night's hunting, then we move in," he replied.

They sat and watched, and when it was almost completely dark, three enormous cave bears came lumbering out from among the rocks and disappeared into the darkness among the trees.

"Now," said Father, "we must hurry."

Quickly, they made their way down the slope. The cave, when they reached it was large and dry and littered with old bones. The bears were not tidy housekeepers.

Mother dropped her bundle and unloaded Two-Eyes. Then she chased Littlenose into the back of the cave and joined Father, who was building a rock barricade across the entrance.

Littlenose was very tired, and he quickly curled up with Two-Eyes and fell asleep.

When he woke again, a blazing fire was burning near the entrance to the cave. The opening was blocked up except for a small space at the top. Littlenose crept forward.

Father was standing looking through the space when he jumped down and shouted: "The bears! Here they come!"

Almost immediately there was a loud snarl, and a bear's head was thrust into the cave. Father banged its snout with his club. It drew back, but another appeared and reached in a huge paw with sharp claws. A shower of stones drove off this one, while a crack on the ear from a well-aimed rock by Mother chased out the third.

And so it went on. The bears tried to get into their cave, while Father and Mother fought to drive them off with sticks and stones and Father's club.

Littlenose got very excited. He picked up a stone and threw it . . . and nearly took Father's nose off!

Father angrily pushed him to the back of the cave out of harm's way. He could still hear shouts and growls coming from the front, and fidgeted impatiently. Then he

noticed something. There was a wide
crack running up one wall and into the roof.
He wondered for a moment, then ran over

and squeezed himself into the crack. It was
really quite easy to climb, and in a few
moments he was in the open air on top of the
rocks.

Littlenose crept forward and looked down.
But so little firelight got past the rocks that he
could see almost nothing.

"A torch," he thought, "that's what I need,"

and scrambled back to the cave.

He found a long thorny branch with a thick bushy mass of leaves and twigs at one end, and lit it in the fire. Neither Father nor Mother noticed.

Back on top of the rocks, he leaned over and held out his torch while peering down. He could see the bears now, hurling themselves at the barricade and squealing and snarling as stones from inside flew round their heads. Littlenose leaned farther out to get a better view – and lost his balance. He managed to grab the rock with both hands, but dropped the torch. In a shower of sparks, it fell to the ground.

As it fell, a well-aimed rock sent one of the bears stumbling backwards. It sat down with a thump, right on the thorny stick, which caught in its fur. Seeing the flames behind it, it leapt forward.

The fire followed, and the bear ran squealing to its two friends.

But they, seeing it apparently being chased by the mysterious fire, ran away.

It ran after them, yelping in fright. They ran even faster.

Away they went until all three were lost to view . . . except for the torch, which bobbed and sparkled in the darkness, until it too disappeared.

Back in the cave, Littlenose found Father dancing round the fire and shouting, "We did it! We did it! We chased them away!"

From inside the cave, he hadn't seen the torch, and thought that he and Mother had done it all by themselves. Littlenose decided it would be wiser not to say anything.

And that is how Littlenose came to move house. The three bears were never seen again, and when Mother had cleared their rubbish out of the cave, it made a snug home.

As the days passed, other members of the tribe began to find caves nearby, and soon almost all of Littlenose's old neighbours were living around him again. In fact, almost nothing was changed. Littlenose was still as naughty as ever, and he still managed to get into the most dreadful scrapes. But that is another story.